ERRATA

JACOB SMULLYAN

© 2016 by Jacob Smullyan

All Rights Reserved.

Printed in the United States of America.
Set in Mrs Eaves XL with LaTeX.

ISBN: 978-1-944697-17-4 (paperback)
ISBN: 978-1-944697-18-1 (ebook)
Library of Congress Control Number: 2016915150

Sagging Meniscus Press
web: http://www.saggingmeniscus.com/
email: info@saggingmeniscus.com

For AM

ERRATA

I

HE world is that which remains when all that is not the case has been subtracted.

The canonical text is the complete account of all that is not the case.

This text is the canonical text.

The previous remark, however, may be erroneous.

II

THERE is an esoteric truth re cupolas. All cupolas are subtly linked. Not that you can go, in one story, suddenly from one to another, but in that any story involving a cupola is itself linked to any other, so that one can create a story from the first half of the first, leading up to the cupola, and the second half of the second, leading away from it, and that story is just as real as the first two. Where cupolas are concerned, any rights to individual existence we posit in ourselves melt away.

III

ZANDER came into P. as the sun tested its paths, verifying their glitter. Whether P. should be described as busy or deserted was difficult to tell. The clear marks of emptiness were not apparent; there were the vehicles, the sounds of people walking somewhere, heads in the crowds. Yet they did not seem to be the people of P., or even people in P.; they were conjoined with it in an ephemeral and unsatisfying mode. Zander doubted whether the man at the counter from whom he asked a coffee would persist long enough to give it to him. That the man did was not reassuring; it seemed merely to confirm a kind of existential prejudice, a dogmatic habit with no ontological foundation.

Zander's coffee, by contrast, offered a familiar impermanence—it evaporated, diminished in volume by being sipped, and grew cold. Zander did not bother to notice that the barista had written "Zander" on the disposable cup.

He had come to the café, not for the beverage, but for what it promised: a moment by himself with the world. Here he could sit, apart from things, and yet in intimacy with them, and think thoughts without having to chase them. Time would be itself for once. And yet he knew that as soon as he tasted the sweetness of Time resting with him, embracing him with its warmth, its promise of infinity, that vessel of plenitude would break and he would return to the pursuit of a retreating reality.

And, as he sipped his coffee and watched the arm of another, apparently perfectly happy, assured, and relaxed customer return another cup to the table after a blissful sip, in perfect synchrony with his own, he realized that it was only in misery, not in bliss, that he was in contact with the world and was, therefore, himself. For when he enacted the ritual of bliss he was no-one, he vanished into a paradigm. The experience was pure simulacrum. When the illusion dissipated and a complete, physical and psychical anxiety took over, filling the space of mind, he was again present even as he agonizingly scrambled after a presence constantly retreating before him.

This is called pleasure.

Whatever it was that Zander watched from the window of the café as he suffered bliss to come and go was not really P.

Whoever it was who watched that which was not really P. through the windows of the café, suffering bliss to be revealed as agony, and vice versa, was not really Zander.

The coffee, perhaps, was really coffee. But only if you mean by that the coffee you don't really mean when you say "coffee." When you say, "I'd like some coffee," you don't mean the coffee Zander was drinking. Names adhere to objects with promise, not to things of the world whose promise has been whored already into nothingness. No, there is no name that would settle for an object of this world. Even when his coffee was fresh, it was no longer the coffee to which his desire had given existence and a name.

IV

I'M not entirely sure that I would know a cupola. It is an object I recognize, if at all, in a shadowy way, without surety. I expect it to be an architectural prominence, with a quasi-spherical aspect. But when a candidate appears, I am never certain whether it is a typical example, whether it really deserves the name. And this means that somehow my story is decoupled from all the others. That special unity that others feel, their stories all linked, their beings grounded in each other, I do not have. Because I am cupola-blind.

By the purest chance, I see my cupola-blindness, which only reveals the possibilities of infinitely many other blindnesses. These blindnesses, should they be, could be taken to mean that there are infinite riches hidden to my sight. But another interpretation rings truer: the train of my continuous story trusts in the foundation of bridge after bridge. But that foundation is less than a dream. With a dream, at least, there is a dreamer. With reality, the nexus that holds it together is nowhere. We are trapped in a prison of nothingness.

When no-one is paying attention, I lift the tablecloth and consider the table leg to my left. I am fairly certain none of the people I fear or respect would agree with me if I asserted—boldly? cheerfully? with deference? with defiance?—that it was a cupola.

Yet, in my heart, can I rule out that it might be one? Is there a Senator in my heart's parliament who will stand up and give a rousing speech, explaining why not? And even if there were, what then? What difference would it make?

V

THEY removed the blindfold only after the long trek on circuitous, mountain roads had given way to miles of flatter highway. For several hours, the cool air had provided evidence that it was night, and when the rag over his eyes was roughly torn away, Z. at first saw nothing. The brigands would not answer his questions—not why he had been taken, so long ago, nor why he was released so suddenly and so in the present. At least, he assumed that this, whatever it was, was what he used to call "present," long ago, before the Night fell, when (he had thought) there was something to present. In his confusion he cried out, "Is this the present?" He could not be sure whether, in the strange mixture of sounds that followed, the laughter of his captors was the predominant ingredient, or the cackling of animals—chickens? hyenas?—or the wind, or the noises of demonic machines. And he heard, or imagined, words buried like fossils in the mingled sounds, like faces in clouds, or like faces. "Where is he, he asks?" he heard, and he thought, "they think I asked—*where* I was present." Another voice, deep and guttural, or was it a loud engine rushing by? rasped out something: "Papa," or "Pisa," or even: "Piss off." The sounds grew faint; only a twittering hiss, the aural equivalent of starlight, surrounded him. Finally his eyes, so unused to discriminating light and dark, or even right and left and up and down, showed him that his world again consisted of regions, distinguished from one another by shades of light, or its absence, which was the same thing.

When this happened, a memory, not of a time or an event, but of a state, like a trace in the body, or a child's first smell of coffee, came to Z.—a memory of "standing." This concept was not one he could define, but he knew it was a feature of the past, like Mama and Papa and like Light, that he felt with his whole being. Light had returned; could it be . . . could he stand?

As Z. lay stretched in the dirt and rubbish behind the truck stop outside (perhaps) Pisa, his eyes neither closed nor open, not knowing whether he lay facing the sky or the ground, he fought to stand, although he did not know what it was to stand. The stump of his left arm shot out and a foot tensed at the end of his leg. It began to rain, and his open mouth filled with mud.

VI

THE old man's glasses glinted with reflections of things true and untrue. The magic lamp of reality flashed and two voices whispered to him, in vehement disagreement, yet in partnership. Years ago he had rebelled against being brought in to mediate their dispute. The passage of decades brought a painfully won détente and the peace of surrender to torment; he realized finally that the only purpose of the dispute was that he mediate it.

Day after day, he lay stretched in the hay as the noises of the world went unheeded. Night after night he sat before his lamp, sifting through the images which flashed before him in the darkness, images of the substrata of the world, deep truths and deep lies. And patiently he coped with the tiresome debate, his fingers at his beads.

VII

BRIGHT, colorful days! When the terminus would open up to a high, painted ceiling, and the stones be warm. When children, if there were any, would rush in excitedly, their hearts completely taken with some fond nonsense. When the choice of red shirt and red socks would have no sense of irony or compensation.

Z. smiles at the old folk as they hobble by; he is rushing, but amiably, with no anxiety. There is no line at the ticket counter. The train (bright! red!) is ready, and not too full.

Z. feels himself sliding forwards into the inevitability of the future. The smiling children were all about him; now they are behind in the dark and their high voices are growing faint.

There is a pain in his chest, just a little one, as the train begins to move. *Oh God,* he cries to himself—*Where have I been? Where am I going?*

VIII

It had been many years that S. had lived in a muddle of noise that was also a silence. It was a silence because something was lacking, something for which a space was always provided. A voice was missing, a voice—or was it a noise—no-one seemed to be expecting, yet the space for it was there, and in its absence everyone felt a compulsion to fill it with desultory talk. The truth was, we were all waiting, those of us with S., waiting for something to begin. There was a curtain, but long ago we forgot to face it.

In fact, how do we know the curtain was even drawn? The absence of the voice, the closure of the curtain, these perhaps were merely traditions. Behind us, or next to us, the voice might have been audible all the while, and the curtain, the stage—why, perhaps we were on the stage.

S. was recalling the deal he had made, many years before, with the CIA. A necessary compromise, justifiable because [redacted]. Had he not done so, the outcome could have been far worse. He had told himself this for years. But he was never satisfied.

From the airplane he looked at the great water below, and traced his ancient dissatisfaction to its source. And he heard the voice at last, and knew that his ancient compromise had been quite wrong after all. And that to be at peace with that voice was the only true peace.

The captain saw him looking out at the

water. He put out his cigarette and took a breath of the sea air, and made an eloquent gesture to someone in the belly of the plane, like the motion of a conductor, tracing a hook or a question mark. The rough burlap sack that came over S.'s head was drawn down and tied. It was time. The hatch opened and the wind came in, and S. felt the rushing air fill the silence and hold his spirit up.

IX

SAMUELS was the sort who seemed to have been born wearing a cravat. It was an inpenetrable shield erected between his "self" and the "world," and as such it participated in the unending creation and destruction of both. Kept from embracing one another at every moment, Samuels and his world died lonely, miserable deaths on the colorful noose of his purported dignity and self-assertion.

Samuels knew this very well, yet persisted in his style with a deliberate self-laceration. What little he felt from the world outside was the mellow light of a certain forgiveness—not unmixed with suspicion, ridicule, and pity, but not without a residual radiance of kindness either. Perhaps this was enough for him; perhaps he could not have withstood more.

Every conversation he overheard, as he sipped his latté at the counter, reminded him of capacities for human interaction he did not possess and would probably repudiate if he did; he felt mystification and even pity observing them in others, and some envy mixed with pathos. He would melt and dissolve in the acid of his own pain, were he not protected by the cravat, wrapped tight around him.

X

N. was seeking the infinitessimal, on the theory that the smaller, the richer, the more essential. Every complex, he somehow felt, was an illusion, a source of impurity, or more correctly, a distraction. He wanted to hone his attention to the point that the Given lay there forever under the tree, never to be unwrapped. Yet as soon as he became conscious of the Given, he could not but feel something else that intruded itself into his sensorium—a kind of pleasure that came between himself and the world like a fine mist. And in the mist, he swooned and his mind became dull, if only for an instant, but that instant was enough for his mind to be unmoored, and once again without end he drifted in the sea of images.

XI

FROM his café chair, Z. could observe, with some admiration, the crafty and effective trade in self-satisfaction performed by T., a wily beggar who appeared once or twice a week outside the market. His followers gave him astounding sums of money in exchange for embraces and protestations of love and undying friendship. T.'s face, though, as he turned away from his clients, said something else; if not quite hard, not quite calculating, at least it betrayed a weariness from holding the mask required by his business affairs. How could it not?

This morning, Z. saw one businessman

in an unfashionable suit, with a cravat and red socks, a man clearly out of his element and past his prime, deliver over to T. twenty crowns. Was he an imbecile? A fool? Or a saint? No, none of these; Z. saw, looking into the yellow eyes of the old businessman, staggering away, that he was a realist—and that a realist is one who knows that all human life is founded on illusion. The old man knew that T.'s love was an empty fraud, and yet he handed over money which he could ill afford, and publicly embraced him, knowing all that fully and precisely in the very moment of the embrace.

What is a philosopher, thought Z., what is a seeker after truth, when truth is precisely that which does not need to be sought, and indeed, cannot be? He is a seeker after illusion. The philosopher is one who resists the truth with every fiber and rejects it totally. This is never more true than of the philosopher whose illusion is that he accepts the truth.

And yet, illusion cannot be sought either; it is never elsewhere, where seeking seeks to take us. The philosopher seeks illusion, claiming to seek truth, in the fruitless hope that he will escape from both into the blessedness of a child's dear hope—like a tree wishing to become an acorn.

XII

THE movement of becoming, the submission to the abject convenience of identity, would have characterized Zander's daily mug of joe. But this morning, roused by some emergency and stranded waiting in an alien environment, there was no mug and no joe. What occupied the space of that which was absent?

XIII

A smart party. Pranks played on and on. The furnace of Z's wit withered eyebrows, razed carefully wrought constructions of all sorts: personal loyalties, rivalries, convictions, best wishes.

Without a furnace, Z. cannot be.

With a furnace, Z. cannot be Z.

XIV: The Birthday

S. tolerates a celebration whose diligence is the true sign of its lack of conviction. In fact, no-one truly prefers that he was born, certainly not S. himself. Some are afraid of the potential world without S., just as they are afraid of the world with him. Or rather, as they would be afraid; for there has never been an S., as S. knows very well.

For S., the loathsome day honors his crucifixion, his impalement on the pretense of being. Every gesture made towards him means, exactly: *Slave! you must remain where you are.*

XV: The Attack

THE pain came on quite suddenly, and not in the place where Z. expected it. Not that he expected an attack—indeed, it came as a total surprise. But he found nonetheless, despite not having anticipated being struck in this way, that there was a way he thought it would go, a scenario ready-at-hand as if he had planned or imagined it. And yet, he could not recall ever having thought of this eventuality before. Nonetheless, while part of his mind registered the sensations, now here, now there, that signalled the attack, another part felt reactive emotions (terror, relief . . .) and yet another stood nearby, reasoning, trying to harmonize the warring mental functions, there was still another part remaining, that said, critically: "This does not feel right. Is it not supposed to feel like this, it should feel like so. But why is that?"

The attack passed. Z. spoke of it to no-one. The voice that had revealed itself to him alone was not transferable. And Z. suspected that the attack, and his unease about it, were the same thing.

XVI

As he lay dying in the ditch, a warm breeze wafted over him, grazing his cheek. In that perception was its own embedded thought, that the caress of that breeze had an enormity the frenzied events of his life lacked; that caress, properly, was his substantial life, and the rest, something fleeting, a side-show.

He got on with it.

XVII: A Dream Haunting

WHILE we were laughing over the endearing foibles of my friend X, I was reminded of Y, who also knows him and who in turn has her share of amusing anecdotes told about her. One day towards evening, I ran into Y as she was picking up her car—it seemed it was always being repaired—and she gave us (evidently X was there as well) a lift into K. We parked on a leafy side-street and walked up a steep incline; it was already beginning to get dark. I followed up the hill with some difficulty, and as we turned the corner, suddenly it seemed very dark indeed, almost pitch black, and I found that I had fallen somehow quite far behind and could no longer properly see X and Y in the distance. Moving was difficult and I was now close to the ground, almost crawling. Then I felt, very distinctly, an uncanny presence, as of a ghost; with a thrill of fear, I came to understand precisely what is meant by the expression "my flesh crawled." Turning, I looked up from the sidewalk and saw two men emerge from a tunnel (from a garage, perhaps, or a subway); they wore coats and walked with a ponderous dignity. When they faced me I saw that their faces were not a human color, but literally ashen, if slightly purpled—they might have been made of a ceramic material. The terrible shock I then experienced was not, however, merely from the fact that these figures were clearly not human—a relatively minor disturbance that just served to pry my mind from the all-encompassing delusion it was stuck on—but from the overpowering realization that followed it: *I did not know, and had never known, any such persons as X or Y.*

XVIII

THERE is no harm, thought Z., in doing such-and-such. Thus harm and such-and-such become inseparably linked for him, and his eyes, rolling around the lake, reflected a horror he could never understand.

Walking into the summer-house, he tried not to notice the satin curtains. The curtains which, had he murdered B. and wrapped her body in them, would still show a slight spotting of blood.

He did not murder B. (There was no B.)

There were no curtains. (There was no summer-house.)

It was not summer. (It is never summer.)

XIX

What those who live in K., famous for its impenetrable fogs, call "the lifting of the fog" is no such thing, as the fog itself is never seen to lift; a noble gas, it reacts to nothing. Yet it cannot be denied that there are experiences and memories of K. without it. One afternoon, Sanders may turn his head to look at Y, and the bright sun, unimpeded, fills the field, and the sounds of children are not muffled. While this scene lasts, fog is impossible; it could no more be seen to enter than be seen to depart. When it is present, however, it is an ontological necessity, outside of Time; K. could not be K., nor Sanders Sanders, without it.

XX

In F., Y. still appeared in his winter gear while Spring put forth its first shoots; in compensation his coffee today had ice in it. He sat down amidst a gentle clatter of spoons and the talk of frustrated artists and booksellers, and waited for the inner silence to begin, the silence that arose within him in such situations, like a great ancient gate that only appears in the city on high holy days, and is obscured the rest of the time in the middle of the market by posters and ramshackle structures erected by salespeople, fanatics, or derelicts.

As he waited, he saw a man across the café, an old man in tattered clothes, a threadbare tweed jacket, trousers that needed to be belted lightly around his emaciated frame; for shoes he wore filthy bedroom slippers. The old man had his eyes—yellow, slightly bulging—on him; his stare was a kind of fierce but wary disapproval, but its purpose was not merely to disapprove—he, too, was waiting for something. Y. noticed that the cheap coffee in front of the old man, in a styrofoam cup, clearly was not purchased in the café; due to his penury, his presence was tolerated although he was not a customer. Perhaps, thought Y., he and the old man were waiting for the same gate to open, but while they were both waiting, it would open for neither of them. Or, thought Y., the gate they were waiting for would never open, and never had, for truly it was an illusion; there was a gate for them both, but it was waiting for them, not the reverse. Then Y. understood the old man's disapproval; for in Y. waiting for a gate the old man had learned would never open, Y. not only reminded him of the other gate, but summoned it.

XXI

Z. emerged from the doctor with his hand heavily bandaged. It was awkward, if not impossible, for him to extract the coins to pay for his espresso; the girl at the counter heaved a quiet sigh and settled into herself, making the delay more awkward. This annoyed Z. She could have made a more generous gesture, there were several alternatives: simply dismissing him with a smile, telling him to pay another day; offering to help (he wouldn't have minded the fleeting intimacy of her reaching into his coinpurse); even if she were impatient, she might have smiled a little, with a hint of openness. He was instead expected to create his own openness. Is that even possible, he wondered, or would he have to take the openness he needed from somewhere else? What if he ran out of it? Perhaps that is what had happened to her. He could feel his soul become tattered as the dull eyes of the barista looked into his, waiting for his coins to fall into her hands.

He and what remained of his soul made their way to a small table in the corner of the room. He was too injured by the brutal doctor with her experimental yaws therapy and the cold barista to sit anywhere but alongside the wall, where he felt safer. And there he waited for his soul to "feel better," whatever that means.

How much of his life was spent as a spiritual patient, waiting for his soul to finally come into focus and reveal its eternal nature? Was waiting any part of that nature also? If the pain were to stop, really stop and not merely be replaced by an anti-pain, a pain masquerading as an ecstatic pleasure, would he not be impatient for it to start again?

XXII

SAMUELS was not a good judge of other people, it seemed, and had fallen in with the wrong sort, all because in the desert of his soul it seemed like they were the most approachable and he might slake his thirst with them without consequence. The result was three broken ribs. He emerged from the hospital heavily bandaged, with his cravat askew, as the arm motions necessary to tie it were too painful. Just to breathe hurt him terribly. It was unclear which was worse, to breathe in, or to breathe out.

A little better, perhaps, was the space in between. At first it was like the cartoon between movies at a double feature; first a blackness, then a blossoming of the static pain of his injuries, that splashed across the screen in bright colors with a comical violence. But as attractive to the eye as the cartoon of pain was, he could not always, at those moments, pay attention to it; there was a blind spot there and he would fall into it. He would never know or perceive it at the very moment, but from time to time he would see that things had changed around him; a woman's smile was not the smile she had always had, because she no longer loved him; a child was no longer a child; the old man in the newsstand had died and now was replaced by someone new who carried fewer papers, and more gum; the streetcars no longer ran down Main St., and the old hotel had been replaced with twelve condominiums; use of the second person singular ("thou") had fallen out of fashion. From these changes he realized that, in between one stress and another, breathing in and breathing out, something fundamental in the world had been switched, although no one paid any attention to it; Samuels was no longer Samuels; thou wast no longer thou. Had there ever been a hand in Samuels' hand, it would not be his hand that held it, and the hand he held—was it ever thine?

Where art thou, he cried within. *Didst thou fall into that deep hole between one terrible pain and the other, when the cartoon tape ran out on the projector and was flicking forever? Where must I go to find thee?*

XXIII

Z. fell to his knees, quite literally; suddenly incapable of controlling his body properly, he had rolled off the bed and fell hard on his bones. His little son put his arms around him: "Papa, are you all right?"

Is this the moment when time begins to go backwards: when the son comforts the father?

XXIV. Insomnia

AT night Sanders was encumbered with the reality of the terrible note sounding behind everything, a constant and total pain: the volume of his sensations turned up, every inch of space full of voices crying out, somewhat distantly but incessantly, inescapably.

The pain lay not in the voices themselves, he realized, but in their essential distance and the necessity to reach for them regardless.

XXV

Why do we embrace false gods, or bring them at all into the business of shriving our souls?

Because, just as we learn there are no gods, we learn that our souls will never be shriven. One impossibility requires another.

XXVI

S. was not accustomed to the ground, to being close to it. He did not kneel, on cushions or otherwise; he did not squat. He sat properly, on chairs, and stood, and was perhaps not very bendable. The part of himself he was concerned with was the upper part, and the lower supporting structure was a distant affair. The ground was something dirty, to be avoided at all costs. Only in extremis, in the case of severe illness, say, would he and the ground approach one another, as when stricken by poisoned food he crouched in agony by a filthy toilet, or passed out from a wound.

For S. to kneel in his room, alone, then, his head to the dusty floor, his knees aching, was therefore not a matter of exercise.

XXVII. Italian Concerto

A brief, unforgettable, unbearable moment, just before the final phrases: the imaginary soloist's plaintive *melos* attains an ecstatic depth, its forlorn pain and poignant isolation absolute, unreachable. The catharsis of the sublime, we are told by Aristotlean tradition, is tied up with falsity—tragedy is a killed virus that enables us to process pain and safely overcome it. This aspect is undeniable. Yet the coin has another side—the virus of the tragic would mean nothing if it did not only uproot but embody the truth. And the paradox of tragedy ultimately is greater than any pat resolution where layers of representation are kept separate, unlike in reality. For in tragedy, we feel genuine pain and despair, and also joy. When Bach wrote these notes, in faith, he was not pretending or merely employing an ingenious psychological artifice—he shared his heart, which genuinely felt the deepest pain and despair—and also, not orthogonally, the deepest joy. *These are not separate.*

XXVIII

SITTING with his book, S. says to himself, "If only this pain would go away (the pain in my soul), I could begin to read." And that leads to the generalization, "If only the pain in my soul would go away, I could begin to live."

But we should regard any statement of the form "If only X, I could begin to live" as suspect, for the truth is the reverse: "Begin to live, and only then (possibly) X."

It is easy to make a fetish of our pain, as it excuses our lack of joy. Is joy too much trouble? Forced joy could be a sort of torture. The only bliss that is all-encompassing is the total affirmation of life, pain and all.

That is the real force of the tragic: the expression of untrammelled joy.

XXIX. The Cry of Despair

CHRIST'S climactic cry on the cross—*O Father, why hast thou forsaken me?*—is not a fall from the mystical, brought about by the enormity of pain, the weakness of the flesh and its dissolution. On the contrary, it is its apotheosis, going to the very heart of the vision.

Without despair, without the wonder of abandonment, affirmation is not complete, and the embrace is empty. Christ could not be Christ without our despair, and his own.

XXX

In the beginning was pain, and the pain was with God, and the pain was God. All that has been done has been done through pain.

For force is in conflict with force: nothing else is true of force; that is what force is.

Verily, to do is to be in pain. To do without pain is merely to be blind to the victim of the act, to be deaf to the victim's cries of pain or pleasure.

Pain is the fascination of the act, a narrowing of the world leading into a tiny vessel that opens far, far away, where the stars battle openly.

There are two absences: one that conceals, another that reveals.

How can you make visible that which is always before your eyes? By making it disappear.

For our bright eyes have learned to do, not to see. We see the swimmers, not the sea. Yet somewhere in our bodies, the weight of the ocean presses, presses us to extinguishment.

Eventually one realizes that one is being destroyed.

Entertainment is closer than tragedy to what in casual speech we usually call the tragic; it is the pessimistic form which asserts that the truth must be avoided, that we must shift our perspective so that we are diverted by the play of light and shadow, and that a destiny we create within it completes us, albeit temporarily. The other truth, our pain, is erased by the absence that conceals.

Yet with a slight difference of emphasis, the same motion performs the opposite operation: the truth is revealed by having been erased. The brief lifting of our hopes enables us to perceive our vast, unmoving despair.

This is called joy.

The previous remark, however, may be erroneous.

Self-Portrait, 1986. Jacob Smullyan.

Jacob Smullyan (born 1964) is a pianist and the founding editor of Sagging Meniscus Press. His poem cycle about surging muck, *Dribble*, was written in 1983 and published in 2015; his forthcoming novel, *The Sultan of Brisbane*, is concerned with annoying persons. He lives in New Jersey with his wife and children.